For Patrick, who is so very kind
—S.C.

For my mom, with love
—E.U.

An imprint of Rodale Books
733 Third Avenue
New York, NY 10017
Visit us online at RodaleKids.com.

Rodale Kids books may be purchased for business or promotional use
for special sales. For information, please e-mail: RodaleKids@Rodale.com.

Printed in the United States of America
Manufactured 201711

Design by Amy C. King
Text set in Report School
The artwork for this book was created with pencil and paper,
then painted digitally in Adobe Photoshop.

Library of Congress Cataloging-in-Publication Data is on file with the publisher.

ISBN 978-1-62336-878-4 paperback
ISBN 978-1-62336-921-7 hardcover

Distributed to the trade by Macmillan
10 9 8 7 6 5 4 3 2 1 paperback
10 9 8 7 6 5 4 3 2 hardcover

I am Kind

RODALE KiDS

I want to be kind
like my Mom.
She is the kindest
person I know.

She helps Grandma work out.
They walk in the park.

They bend and stretch.

It is fun.

Mom helps strangers, too.
Once a week we go to our town's
community center.

We bake and cook.

We serve the food
to hungry people.

Stan lives next door.
He hurt his arm
and can't garden.
I try to be kind.

I weed and water
his plants.

Stan thanks me with
some strawberries.

How kind!

When the rain comes down,
my umbrella goes up.

I find room
for one more
to be kind.

Maya is a new student
at my school.
Her family just moved to town.

She is my new math partner.

I see Maya
sitting alone at lunch.

My friends and I
ask her to eat with us.

She thanks us
for being kind.

At home
I like to build
big spaceships.

My baby brother likes
to knock them down.

Sometimes it isn't easy
to be kind.
But I find a way.

My troop goes on a nature hike.
Maya joins us.

First, we cross a creek.
We cheer for each other.

Next, we climb a winding path.
Some climb fast. Some climb slow.
I am kind to all.

We reach the campsite.
We take a break.
It's time to eat.
Yum!

We learn about
plants and animals.

It is time to go home.
We pack up everything.
We clean up the site.

We are kind to the earth.

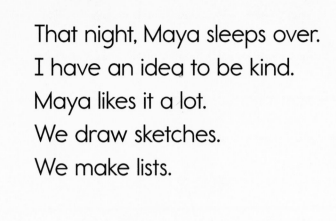

That night, Maya sleeps over.
I have an idea to be kind.
Maya likes it a lot.
We draw sketches.
We make lists.

We tell our plan
to my mom.

She loves it!

We borrow some supplies from Stan.

He loves our idea, too.

We go shopping with my mom.
We buy a few more supplies.

We get to work.
I dig holes.
Maya plants the flowers.
We work hard.

At last, we are done. Now everyone
can enjoy our surprise.

It is the best feeling
when I am kind.

How can YOU be kind?

Can you think of three examples?

Also available:

I Am Thankful

Look for these other titles in the
POSITIVE POWER series:

- **I Am Brave**
- **I Am Strong**
- **I Am Smart**
- **I Am Helpful**

To learn more about Rodale Kids Curious Readers,
please visit RodaleKids.com.

31901062724176